Will You Be My Friend?

The first book of the
"Two Sisters Pumpkin Patch" book series.

Written By:

Karen L. Clarke

Illustrated By:

Kat South

"Inspired by our friends at
Two Sisters Pumpkin Patch in Mount Sterling, Kentucky"

About the Author: Karen L. Clarke

I live in Owingsville, Kentucky with my wonderful husband and four amazing children. I have always loved to write but this is the first time I have had the courage to share what I have written. I love this story for so many reasons! I love Two Sisters Pumpkin Patch. It is such a peaceful place, and the animals are taken care of so well. Of course, the place and the animals would not be what they are if not for the great Webb family pouring their hearts into it daily. Thank you, A.C. and Susie, for sharing your beautiful farm with me. Thank you, Alecia and Andrea, for spending hours in the barn with my kids and me, letting us get to know each animals' unique personality, and especially for sharing sweet Ruby with us from her very first day on the farm. Finally, thank you for believing in me and encouraging this book. I could not have done it without you! To the wonderful illustrator, Kat: thank you for turning my story for children into a book for children. I am so proud of you, Kat!

About the Illustrator: Kat South

Kat was thirteen years old when she was asked to illustrate this story. Although she has been drawing since she was eleven, she had never drawn animals before, except for the occasional cat. The first drawing of Ruby in this book was the first cow she had ever drawn. It is followed by the first dog she ever drew, then the first donkey, the first goat, the first chicken, and the first goose! Art is one of Kat's God-given talents. Kat is now fourteen years old and will surely publish many more art projects in the future

Early one spring morning, Sapphire the cow gave birth to twin calves. While this should have been a very happy occasion, it actually made Sapphire quite sad. She knew she was only able to care for one of the twins. She was a young mother and only had enough milk for one calf to thrive. She knew if she tried to split her milk between the two calves, neither would get enough and then both might die.

The boy calf was much larger and stronger. Sapphire knew that she could take care of him. The girl calf was smaller and weak. Sapphire knew that she would need extra help to grow up to be a strong cow. Sapphire told the little girl calf that she could not take care of her, so she would have to leave her there. She told her to just wait right where she was, because Sapphire knew that a nice lady named Alecia would be coming by very soon.

"Alecia comes by every morning to check on all of the animals. I am sure when she sees you here alone, she will take you up to the most beautiful part of the farm and take care of you there. One time, I even saw her take in a scraggly, skinny little dog that has no business on a farm. She will certainly take you in, too! She lives on that beautiful part of the farm, and her parents and sister do, too. They call the farm Two Sisters Pumpkin Patch, and in the fall, thousands of people come to visit. You will love it there," explained Sapphire.

With tears in her eyes, Sapphire said goodbye to her lovable new calf. Sure enough, less than half an hour later Alecia came walking by, just like Sapphire had said.

"Well, look at you!" said Alecia. "You are such a small, sweet baby. You should not be here all alone. I guess your mommy couldn't take care of you. Don't you worry, little calf! I will take you to my barn and I will take care of you. There are a lot of other animals there. You will be happy with us!"

Alecia finished checking on the rest of the cows, then put the new calf in her truck and headed to the barn. The new calf was the most beautiful red and white calf Alecia had ever seen! When they finally arrived at the barn, Alecia's parents and sister were there doing their morning chores.

"What did you bring home now?" asked Alecia's dad.

"I think I will call her Ruby!" Alecia replied.

Ruby was curled up all alone on the grass nearby. Andrea and Susie, Alecia's sister and mom, walked over to meet her. They both agreed that Ruby the calf was the most beautiful red color they had ever seen.

"Ruby it is!" Alecia announced.

Ruby liked her new name, and her mom was right—this part of the farm was beautiful and clean and peaceful. Ruby knew she would be very happy here. She could tell that the family loved all of the animals, and it was clear that the animals loved the family, too. Alecia fed Ruby some delicious milk from a bottle and fixed her a nice pen in a cozy shelter with plenty of straw for a bed.

Ruby was excited to see so many different kinds of animals and she couldn't wait to make new friends. By the time she was settled in to her new home, though, it was getting late. Her adventure would have to wait until tomorrow! Ruby fell asleep that night thinking that she was the luckiest calf in the world. Such a nice lady had rescued her and given her a new home, and tomorrow she would get to make so many new friends.

Shortly after the sun came up the next morning, Ruby was awakened by a small wet nose sniffing all over her.

"Oh, hello!" said Ruby. "What… I mean WHO… are you?"

"Ahhhem! I am Hobie. I am a very special, very rare, very highly desired type of dog, and I am Alecia's BEST friend. The question is, who are YOU, and why are you here?"

"My name is Ruby, and I am Alecia's friend, too! She rescued me. Did she rescue you, also?" asked Ruby with excitement in her voice.

"Well, yes, she did rescue me," said Hobie quietly. Then, in a much louder, bolder voice he said, "But now we are the very best of friends."

"That's great!" Ruby exclaimed. "Since you are Alecia's friend—"

"BEST friend!" Hobie interrupted rudely.

"Yes, BEST friend, and since I am Alecia's friend, too, will you be my friend?" Ruby asked.

"Ha ha ha ha! Ho ho hee hee hee ha ha ho! Oh, that is funny!" Hobie laughed. "Of course I will not be your friend! I live in the house. I am not friends with animals that live in the barn!"

With that, Hobie turned and shuffled out of the barn to find Alecia.

As she watched Hobie leave, Ruby noticed that a large white goat with horns and piercing brown eyes was staring at her and shaking his head as if he was disgusted to see Ruby there. Ruby decided right away that she would stay away from the goat and try to forget about Hobie. After all, there were plenty of other animals she could be friends with at the farm!

As Ruby walked through the barn on her way to explore her new home, she saw a chicken outside eating her breakfast.

"Good morning!" Ruby called to the chicken. "I am new here and I was wondering if you would like to be my friend."

"Will I be your friend? Hmm. I don't know. Wait here," said the chicken. She went and gathered the other chickens and asked, "well, what do you think, girls? Should we be friends with that calf?"

"I don't know," responded one chicken. "She is different from any of the other animals in the barn."

"She kind of smells funny," replied another chicken.

Finally, the oldest chicken of the bunch walked over to Ruby and said, "Look, I understand that you want to make friends, but you need to look somewhere else. We are chickens! We are friends with chickens and we have no reason to be friends with a new animal that is so different from every other animal in the barn. Good day!" With that, the old chicken turned away and walked back to the other chickens.

Ruby hung her head and walked away. Once again, Ruby noticed the enormous goat staring at her. He looked even more disgusted than he had earlier when he caught Ruby talking to Hobie.

Ruby laid down in the sunshine and wondered if she would ever have a friend. She looked up and noticed a large family of geese splashing and playing in the pond. She thought that they looked so fun and beautiful! She began to walk down the hill towards the pond. She couldn't help but notice yet again what a wonderful place this was. Suddenly, she could no longer contain her excitement, she was so excited that she took off running towards the geese and yelling at them. "Hellllooooo, beautiful geese! This is so fun! Come and run and jump with me!"

The geese just stood and looked at her, so Ruby slowed down and got a little closer.

"Excuse me, geese. Will any of you be my friend?" asked Ruby.

"Oh! No no no no no no. We are far too busy taking care of our very large family. We do not have time to be your friend," replied the mother goose. "Come along now, children!" With that, the goose family swam off.

Ruby was not so happy anymore. She turned to walk back to the barn at the top of the hill. As she looked up, she noticed the big goat glaring down at her. He was once again shaking his head in disgust. Ruby thought to herself that the big mean goat must be scaring off all the other animals. That might be why no one wanted to be her friend. He clearly was ashamed to have her on the farm.

As Ruby walked back to the barn, she noticed a cat who seemed really nice.

"Will you be my friend?" asked Ruby quietly.

The cat did not respond. Ruby moved a little closer and asked her question again. "Will you please be my friend? I am new here and feeling a little—"

The cat interrupted Ruby.

"Are you talking to me? I am a cat. Cats are not friends with anyone. I look out for myself, I hunt for myself, and I entertain myself. I simply do not need any friends."

With that, the cat turned and haughtily strutted out to the hay field.

Ruby was very sad. She went back into the barn and lay down feeling very unwanted. Before long, Alecia came in and fed Ruby her bottle. Alecia was kind, and Ruby really enjoyed the time she got to spend with her. Yet even though Alecia fed Ruby, pet her, and made her feel loved, Ruby couldn't help but crave the friendship of other animals who lived in the barn with her. Alecia finished feeding Ruby and cleaned her pen, then said good-bye and went to finish the rest of her chores. As soon as Alecia was gone, the giant goat with the piercing eyes came stomping in the barn. Ruby quickly ran out and caught up with Alecia, who was feeding the donkeys.

When the donkeys finished eating, Ruby walked over to a younger donkey, who was about the same size as her.

"I heard Alecia call you Clover," Ruby said to the young donkey. "That's a great name! My name is Ruby. Will you be my friend?"

"Sure!" replied Clover. "My real name is Clover Joe. They just call me Clover for short. So, what would you like to do, new friend?"

Ruby was so happy! She had almost given up on ever making a friend.

Just as Ruby began to answer Clover, his mom, Posie, came running over separated the two.

"Absolutely not, young man! You will not be her friend! Why, she isn't even a donkey! You have a lot to learn, mister!" said Posie in a huff.

This time as Ruby walked away, the big goat wasn't just staring at her. He was also shaking his head and stomping his foot. He snorted and made the same disgusted look he made before, as Ruby ran past him to her safe pen in the barn. She spent the rest of the day there, curled up as tightly as she could in the corner, in hopes that no one would bother her there.

A few hours later, Alecia came in to feed Ruby her last milk bottle of the day. Ruby wouldn't even drink it. She was simply too sad. Alecia patted her on the head and scratched her ears.

"You don't have to drink it tonight if you're not hungry. You have had a big day. I will be back first thing in the morning. Maybe you will be hungry then," Alecia said.

Ruby thought to herself that she would not be there in the morning. She was tired of not fitting in. She planned to run away after everyone fell asleep.

That night when Ruby thought the other animals were sleeping, she began to leave. When she stepped out of the barn, she noticed it was really quite dark and there were scary noises. Besides, where was she going to go? She ran back inside and once again curled into a tight ball in her corner of the barn. She began to cry. She was so lonely, but she was too scared to leave. She didn't know what to do, so she just kept crying.

As Ruby was crying, she heard heavy footsteps heading in her direction. As they came closer and closer, she tried to stop crying but just couldn't. She squeezed her eyes shut as tightly as she could. The footsteps still kept coming closer, and then they sounded like they were in her pen! Ruby was shaking with fear. Finally, she felt warm breath on her forehead so she slowly opened her eyes and saw HIM! It was HIM— the big, scary, mean goat! Ruby jumped to her feet in alarm.

"I'm sorry! I am so sorry. I know you think I am disgusting and I know that no one wants to be my friend and that I shouldn't even be here. I will run away as soon as the sun comes up. Just, please don't hurt me!" said Ruby.

The goat stepped a little closer and said in a soft voice, "You will not run away."

"I promise I will! I promise! I know I don't belong here," cried Ruby.

The goat interrupted Ruby and then, much to her surprise, said, "Ruby, will you be my friend?"

Ruby stopped crying but she still could not look up at the goat.

"My name is Cooper. Will you please be my friend?" said the goat.

Ruby picked up her head and said, "I don't understand. I have asked everyone here to be my friend. They all said no. Every time I talked to one of the other animals, I saw you shaking her head like you were ashamed I had even asked them, like I just don't belong here."

"Oh, Ruby," said Cooper. "Things are not always as they seem! You did not disgust me at all. I was saddened and angry at my farm family. Mostly, though, I was disappointed in myself. You see, I am the oldest and wisest animal on this farm. The others here look up to me as the leader of our farm family, and I have failed them by not teaching them God's Word. Because of that, I have failed you, too. Ruby, the Bible teaches us that God wants all of us to treat each other as friends. It doesn't matter that you look different than everyone else here. You are beautiful because you are just as God made you. You are perfect, actually! God does not make mistakes and since he made you, that means you are perfect, too!"

Ruby held her head high and listened to every word Cooper said. He explained to her that even though God doesn't make mistakes, people and animals do. He said that God expects us to forgive them for their mistakes, and to treat them with love and kindness.

Ruby and Cooper stayed up all night long talking. She loved listening to Cooper talk about God and how He created everything that was beautiful and good in the world. Ruby's favorite part was how God has a perfectly designed plan for each and every one of our lives, and that even though He designed each of us to be unique, He wants us to work together with our differences to glorify Him!

"How do we glorify God?" asked Ruby.

"It's easy! The Bible tells us how to put God first in our life and to love yourself and others," Cooper explained, and then he began to quote Matthew 22:37-38 which says,

"Love the Lord your God with all your heart and all your soul and all your mind. This is the first and greatest commandment. The second is like it: love your neighbor as yourself."

Just then, the rooster crowed. Ruby jumped up and shouted, "This is another day that the Lord has made for us! Come on, Cooper! Let's rejoice and be glad in it, and share the great news with all of the others!"

"You catch on quick!" replied Cooper with a smile. "God loves you and has a very special plan for you. Just promise to trust him always."

"I do, I do!" exclaimed Ruby. "Now, let's go! We must tell the others this great news!"